Julie
AND THE
FIXER UPPER

A Lake Sterling Romance

AMY SPARLING

Chapter One

Romance is for schmucks. You heard me correctly. Romance is for all the people too moon-eyed and stubborn to realize it'll all fall apart in their face one day. Romance gets you nowhere. Snarking on romance, however, will get you *everywhere*.

Assuming you're any good at it.

The navigation app on my phone tells me to turn left. I slow my old Jeep down to a crawl, wondering where exactly the left turn is, finally finding it tucked away in the thick brush of trees that line this old Texas county road. Eyes on the rear-view mirror, I check to make sure the rented box trailer hitched to my car stays there. It's all I have left after my life exploded and I can't lose it. I've never towed anything before, much less all of my precious belongings in an ugly rented box that's not even the least bit aerodynamic. The guy at the rental place warned me not to take sharp turns, so I've spent this entire ten-hour trip worried that the trailer and my Jeep will go tumbling into the ditch each time there's a bend in the road.

So far, so good. And now I'm almost here. Almost *home*.

The last year of my life has been a total disaster. Living in the city didn't help one bit, because when you're in a depressed funk, it's no fun seeing a million other people living their best lives all day long. Who am I kidding? It was no fun seeing *one* person live his best life. In the same apartment complex.

Jason ruined our engagement with his affair, but then he ruined my living situation by shacking up with his new girl in the same downtown apartment complex. Just one hallway over. Then he ruined my career.

It took me ten years to become a recognized name in the romance industry. I poured my soul in to my romance novels, breathing life into my fictionalized characters, dreaming up swoony romances, and giving my readers couples to root for. I even had a TV network negotiating the rights to adapt my six book city romance series into a cute, romantic television show.

The day I discovered Jason was cheating on me was the day I realized I couldn't write romance anymore. I wanted to. My livelihood depended on the money I get from writing. But I just couldn't. The wool over my eyes had been removed, revealing the truth—that all that sappy, silly romance I had once loved was just a lie.

I shake my head. I won't think about all that I lost. I will only look forward and focus on what I have right now. I catch sight of myself in the rear-view mirror and grin. After weeks of looking for the perfect place to live, I finally found it. The GPS says I'm 2.3 miles away from my new home. My dream home.

Butterflies light up in my stomach as I drive down the small road, which is flanked on either side by thick trees. I roll down my window and take in the clean, crisp air. It's a stark difference from the exhaust-filled city air I'm used to. I breathe in deeply, catching sight of my hair in the mirror as it whips around my face.

I had the same boring hairstyle forever, long and straight just like Jason liked it, until a week ago when I got it cut into long layers with light brown highlights to give more definition to my otherwise boring brown hair.

My friends called it a breakup haircut. It's not a breakup haircut, though. It's the haircut a woman gets when she's finally living for herself.

As I drive further down this small road, the thick pine trees part, revealing the hidden beauty of Lake Sterling. The photos online haven't done it justice. It takes my breath away. The afternoon sun glimmers on the deep blue water. The lake is dotted with cottages, all waterfront properties with big back yards, plenty of room around them so you're not too close to the neighbors. I don't need the GPS to find my new home now; I've spent days staring at its picture online.

The white cottage has one bedroom with an extra studio space that I'll use for an office, an open floor plan, and a huge wraparound back porch that faces the water. Little stepping stones lead from the driveway to the front door, and lush, vibrant flowers decorate front of the small home. It is a picture-perfect home. It should be on postcards and puzzles.

I park, trying not to stress about how I'm going to back out of the small gravel driveway with this box trailer attached to my Jeep. I went the entire trip without going in reverse, and I'm not even sure how to take it off the trailer hitch thingy on the back of my car. There's a rental return place located a few miles away in the small town of Sterling, so I'm hoping to unload my stuff and get it turned in tomorrow morning.

My heart races as I step out and stretch my legs,

gazing up at the gorgeous place that is now my own for the next two years. Snagging this rental property was a miracle. Sterling, Texas was voted one of the most charming small towns last year, and it shows. The real estate here sells for way more than it would anywhere else, and homes rarely ever come up for sale or rent. The people who live here, love it here.

As much as I loathe my ex, Jason did do something good for me. All the anger and pain I felt during our breakup might have ruined my romance writing career, but it started me on the path to a brand new journey. I was kind of joking when I pounded out an entire anti-romance novel in just fifteen days—a record for me—throwing all my bitter emotions into my made up character, Private Investigator Rosa Ramirez, the man-hating vixen who seeks out and destroys men who cheat on their partners. But my agent loved it and sold it to a publisher just days later—another record for me.

The first book in my Love Sucks series became an instant bestseller and my publisher wanted me to make it into a series. I just got a massive book advance for the next three books, which gave me the money to plunk down two years' worth of rent at once, which put me in the running to rent my dream home, a small cottage on the lake. I know a dozen other people were hoping to get it, but it's mine now. All mine.

I close my eyes and breathe in deeply, inhaling the sweet scent of the flowers, the crisp spring air, the woodsy pine trees.

"Well, hello, darlin'. What brings you to Sterling?"

The unexpected, somewhat gravelly voice startles me. I yelp, turning around. The woman smiling at me looks to be in her sixties, with bright red lipstick and dark black hair piled into a messy bun on top of her head.

Not everyone in Texas talks like that. I would know, I was born and raised in Dallas and I have never once called someone *darlin'*.

"I'm, uh," I swallow then force a smile and gesture toward my new house. I want to belong here, blend into small town life away from the hustle of the city. Now that I'm here talking to a local, I'm worried she'll know I don't fit in. "I'm new here. I'm moving in today."

"Well then, *welcome*, my dear. I didn't even know the house was ready to be rented!" She holds out her hand. When I go to shake it, she pulls me in for a hug that smells like floral perfume and coffee. "I'm Lina. I live down the road on the left. Blue house, white door. I like to take a walk each evening. Keeps me fit," she says, finally releasing me.

"Nice to meet you."

"I'll let 'cha get back to it," she says, waving as she starts to walk away. "You holler if you need anything, hun."

My landlady lives in Arizona, so we've only communicated through phone and email. She told me the keys would be under a decorative turtle figurine on the back porch. Excitement pulses through me as I make my way across the beautifully green grass yard and into the back yard. I never had a yard in Dallas. It was just concrete as far as you could see.

I step up on to the back porch and gaze out at the lake in front of me. This is stunning. Beautiful. Perfect. I picture sitting out here, sipping coffee and writing my books to the morning sunrise, the sound of birds and nature keeping me company while I fall into my fictional world with P.I. Rosa Ramirez.

I do a little dance on my new back porch. I close my eyes and wiggle and shake, letting loose back here because no one can see me anyway. Just months ago, my life felt like a tragedy. Now I'm thriving. This is my place, in my own little slice of heaven. Jason is a distant memory. In fact, all men are a distant memory.

My dancing is interrupted by the sound of the back door opening.

"Uh... hello?"

My mouth goes dry.

Dirty blonde hair, messy and curly, a scruffy beard, muscles. Muscles for days.

It takes a second for my brain to put all the gorgeous pieces into place, to register that this very attractive man is staring at me, a twist of confusion on his handsome face.

It's only a second, and I'm snapped back to reality. It doesn't matter how good he looks.

There's a man in my house.

Chapter Two

"Who are you?" My voice is too high-pitched, too mousy and scared. I'm supposed to be a strong, independent woman. Not someone who shrieks back in fear. I stand up straighter, channeling my fictional, sassy P.I. "Are you trying to rob the place? Because I haven't even moved in yet so there's nothing to steal."

The man steps onto the porch, lifting an eyebrow as he looks me up and down. "I think you have the wrong address."

"No, I definitely don't. You need to leave or I'll call the cops."

He chuckles.

My hands slap onto my hips. I *think* this is a power pose, but I'm not so sure. There's something about being in this guy's intense stare, his light brown eyes seeming to shoot waves of fluttery electricity thought me that makes it hard to focus.

"Trespassing is not funny!"

He tilts his head. "It's a little bit funny, especially when I'm not the one doing it."

"You *are* the one doing it," I snap.

He chuckles again. "What address are you looking for? I can help you find it."

"I don't need any help. I am right where I need to be." I tug my purse off my shoulder, set it on the wooden porch railing and dig through it. When I find the papers I'm looking for, I hold them up triumphantly. "I have a signed lease."

"I do, too," he says.

"No, you don't."

He grins. "You want to see it?"

I nod. Then I follow him into the house. Into *my* house. Only...

My blood runs cold with humiliation as I look around the place. It's basically a messy construction zone. Plastic tarps cover the floors, power tools litter the kitchen. Gallons of paint sit on a drop cloth in the corner. Oh no.

My jaw drops. "This isn't my house."

My house was a little outdated, but it was all put together in the online listing photos. This house is someone's renovation project. I'm in the wrong house! My fictional P.I. Rosa would have never made this mistake.

"I'm sorry," I say quickly, turning and rushing out of the back door. I jog across the porch, down the three steps, and run back to my car, my heart pounding rapidly. How could I have been so stupid?

My cheeks are burning and are probably pinker than the flowers in the front yard as I start up my Jeep and throw it into reverse. The tires roll backwards and the trailer jets off crookedly, shaking my car as its wheels veer off the driveway and into the yard.

"Crap," I say, shifting into drive. I pull forward a bit, then try to back out again.

This is so not happening. The stupid trailer keeps going off the driveway, rolling into the grass every time I reverse. My heart is racing and I'm freaking out. I'm about to ask Siri to show me videos of how to drive with a trailer on your car when there's a tap on my window.

I roll down my window and put on the fakest smile in the world. But fake-smiling is better than crying, right? "I'll be out of here in just a second," I say.

"You dropped this." Mr. Handsome No Name holds up my lease.

"Great, thanks," I say, quickly taking the papers

and throwing them in my passenger seat. "You can go now. I have this under control."

"There's a problem." He runs a hand through his hair. "The address on your lease is the right address. But I also have a signed lease for this house. My lease is up in June. I'm renovating the house in exchange for free rent."

This new revelation only helps ease my humiliation a teensy tiny bit. But it also brings with it a whole new set of problems.

"But my lease starts *today*, in April. How can we have leases that overlap each other?"

He shrugs, tapping his fingers to the roof of my Jeep. "We need to call Kelly."

"Great idea." I take my phone from the cupholder and scroll for my landlady's phone number.

"While you do that, get out," he says, stepping backward. He opens my car door.

"Excuse you?"

"Get out real quick," he says, motioning for me to move. Then his eyes meet mine and he seems to have a sudden realization. "Please."

I don't even ask why when I climb out of my own car.

"I'm Max, by the way," he says before getting into the driver's seat.

"Julie," I say.

He smiles, then closes the door and expertly backs my car out of the driveway. He pulls forward on the road, then reverses the Jeep and the trailer into the driveway so it'll be easier for me to leave next time I rush out in a hurry.

Kelly answers the phone with a, "Kelly speaking, how may I help you?"

"Hi, this is Julie Baskins. I just rented a property from you in Sterling?"

"Oh, sure, what's up?"

"There's another guy living here. Max? He claims his lease is up in June even though my lease starts today."

"Oh my goodness," she says with a laugh.

Max gets out of my Jeep and tosses me the keys.

On the phone, Kelly is still laughing. "I can't believe I did that. How funny!"

I palm my forehead. She and I have very different ideas of what funny is.

"Speaker?" Max whispers. I nod and put the call on speakerphone, holding out so he can hear.

"So what should we do?" I say.

"I'll just cancel your lease and refund you the deposit. I'm sorry for the mix-up!"

"No!" I say, sounding desperate and pathetic. But I am desperate. "I don't want to lose the house," I add.

"Max can't move out until he's finished with the renovations. I'll tell you what—I'll just refund your first two months' rent and then you can move in when he's gone. Okay? I have another call coming in, so I have to go. Bye now!"

The call ends. My stomach drops.

"What am I supposed to do now?" I say, taking a deep, deep breath to avoid panicking. "There are no hotels within an hour from here. I already gave up my old apartment. My family lives in Florida! My trailer rental is due back tomorrow. I have nowhere to go."

Max shrugs. "Just stay here."

"No way. You could be a weirdo!"

"*You* could be a weirdo," he retorts.

I roll my eyes. "I'm not a weirdo."

"I'm not either."

I heave a heavy sigh.

Max pats my shoulder then steps back. "Just stay in the house with me. I've been sleeping in the studio room anyhow, so the master bedroom can be all yours. It's already been painted so it's ready to move in."

I stare at him, hoping that if I just watch him long enough, I'll know what to do. I have never lived with a guy. Of course, this isn't some kind of romance thing.

It's just a weird coincidence. I won't even have to acknowledge him if I don't want to. I'll just stay in my bedroom until he's gone.

"Call your mom," I say, thinking on my feet just like Rosa would do.

He lifts an eyebrow, but he doesn't question me. He takes a phone from his jeans pocket, touches the screen, and then holds it out to me. *Mama* is on the screen, and it's ringing.

I put the phone to my ear. "Hey, Son," the voice on the other line says. "What's going on?"

"This isn't Max," I explain. "I'm... Max's friend."

"Oh? Gosh, is everything okay?"

"Max is fine. I just wanted to ask if he's a good guy? Trustworthy? Ethical?"

"Of course he is," she says, sounding like she's smiling. "I raised a great man. Quite the gentleman, if you ask me. And... why are you asking me?"

I can't help but smirk while Max watches me, his teeth digging into his bottom lip. He can only hear one side of this conversation, after all.

"He's living in the house I just rented while he renovates it, and he said I could stay here while he works. I have nowhere else to go so I just need to know how safe it'll be."

"He'll take good care of you, dear. You get my

number from him and you call me anytime, okay? I live here in town. I'll come smack my son if he does anything that annoys you."

I laugh. "Thank you, ma'am."

When the call is over, I hand Max's phone back to him.

"Well?" he says.

I bite the inside of my mouth to stop myself from realizing how handsome he is. I shrug. It's not like it matters. "Guess we're roomies."

Chapter Three

My junior high self must be cringing right now. Young Julie thought *she* was awkward? She hasn't even seen how awkward adult Julie can get. I've never lived with a man. My ex, Jason, lived in the same building so we were always together, but I still got to go home each night. He didn't see me in my embarrassing baggy T-shirt pajamas and had no idea I look like a wet dog after showering because my hair gets curly until I straighten it. I worked really hard to be cool and effortless and beautiful around him.

My old mattress was too heavy and awkward to bring to my new place, so I bought one of those foam mattresses that come rolled up in a box that's easier to manage. After Max and I decided to live together, we called our landlady back and worked it out. I don't have to pay rent until Max moves out. It's a good deal financially, but a weird deal overall. This is not how I pictured my first day in my dream home.

Still, I'm going to make the best of it. Max goes back to working on the kitchen and I open the back door of my box trailer, staring at all the contents. I downsized a lot to move here, selling all of my furniture and any big possessions, so I wouldn't have to move them. I could have hired movers, but I wanted to do this on my own. It's a fresh start.

I take a deep breath and reach for the box with my mattress in it.

"Let me help," Max says, his voice so sudden and unexpected that I yelp and hit my head on the short trailer roof.

"Sorry," he says, somewhat bashfully. "Is your head okay?"

"I'm fine." I roll my eyes. "I don't need help."

I go back to the mattress box, grabbing the perforated handle and dragging it out of the trailer. Max stands in the driveway, watching me. "What?" I say, standing up straight and trying not to let it show that I'm out of breath after only a few seconds with that box.

"I don't mind helping," he says.

I shake my head. "Don't you have renovations to do?"

He holds up his hands in surrender, and I feel a little bad. I have to remind myself just because the last man in my life was a complete lying backstabbing jerk, doesn't mean they all are. But I still don't have to be nice to this guy. His mere presence is ruining my new life adventure. I wanted to do this alone. I was supposed to do this alone. He just needs to go away so I can stand in the driveway and pout a bit.

I watch him head back into the house. Once the sound of his power tool cranks back on, I lug the mattress box up to the front porch and then drag it inside, sliding it all the way down the short hallway and into my bedroom. This small cottage has my room on one end, with the bathroom next door, then a hallway to the living room/kitchen open space, and then the small studio space and laundry room on the other side of the house. That's one bit of good news—Max will be sleeping as far away from me as you can get. Good.

I break a sweat carrying in all my boxes and bags of clothes, but I managed to load them up all by myself and I manage to bring them into the house all by myself. *Girl power*, I think as I wipe sweat from my brow. All I have to do is pretend that Max is a piece of furniture that will be leaving shortly. No big deal. This can still be my dream house and my big new start.

In my bedroom, I look around at Max's completed handiwork. The walls are a beautiful denim blue with crisp white trim around the windows and flooring. The original listing online featured boring white paint throughout the house, so this is definitely an improvement, but would have been even better if my landlady had told me about it.

The wooden floors are shiny and clean. I picture rolling out a plush rug under my bed frame to keep the chill off my toes on winter mornings. Of course, I'll need a rug, and a bed frame. For now, it's just a mattress on the floor until I find a bed to buy and have delivered locally.

I open the box, roll out my mattress, and watch in awe as the foam fluffs up to its full size. I unpack the rest of my stuff. I have a couple boxes of home décor items, which I keep in the hallway, but everything else is for my bedroom and office. Since my office will be delayed until Max moves out, I leave those boxes in the hallway too. For now, all I need to write my books is my laptop, day planner, and the gorgeous view outside.

With my clothes hung up in the closet, and my IKEA dresser and nightstand put back together, I make quick work of unpacking everything. My bed is made even if it is just a mattress on the floor right now. The TV is meant for the living room but since that place is a construction zone nightmare, I'll just set it up in my room for now.

"Knock knock," Max says from the hallway.

"Come in." *He's a piece of furniture*, I tell myself. *Don't let his crazy good looks get you all flustered.*

"I … can't."

I glance up from behind my dresser where I've just plugged in my television. The hallway is filled with boxes and garbage bags full of clothes, stacked so high Max can't get around them.

"Just kick that black bag out of the way," I tell him.

He nudges it with his foot. The tall contractor-sized trash bag falls forward. The hair tie I'd hastily used to close it up slips off. The next few seconds pass in slow motion as I watch all of my underwear and bras —both the cute ones and ratty old ones that should have been thrown out years ago—tumble out of the bag and slide across the shiny, varnished floor.

"Crap, I'm sorry," he says, bending to start picking things up.

"No!" I say, standing up so fast I get dizzy. I scramble across the floor, arms splayed out as if my bony fingers can somehow cover up this big, huge mess from his field of vision.

"I'll get it."

"I knocked it over, so I'll help clean it up," he says.

"No!" I grab his forearms, pressing him backward into the door frame. His skin is warm, his muscles taut under my grip. I stare at his chest to avoid his eyes. "That's a bag of my... under clothings..." I say, suddenly finding myself unable to say the words *bra* or *panties*. "You do not need to be anywhere near them."

He chuckles, then takes a step back. "Got it. And sorry for the mess."

I stand up straight, a futile attempt to hide the mess behind me because Max is so much taller than I am. Still, I have to try something. Those are my *unmentionables* all over the floor. And like ninety percent of them aren't very cute. I dress for comfort, not style.

"Do you need something?"

He's a piece of furniture, I repeat in my head. A talking, walking, super attractive piece of furniture.

He scratches the back of his neck, which ruffles his slightly-too long wavy blond hair. It's a good look on him.

"I've been debating how to tile the backsplash in the kitchen," he says. "I have a few color choices and Kelly doesn't care how it's done. You want to pick which one you like the best?"

Oh, right. Renovation stuff. I wish I could reach into my own brain and slap it for being so ridiculously dumb. I am literally anti-romance now. I can't let one guy turn my thoughts to mush. He'll be out of here soon, and I'll forget all about him.

"Sure," I say, happy to get out of this room and this hallway and far, far away from the mess on the floor.

I'm more of a big picture kind of woman. If my house is clean and smells nice and has everything I need, I don't really care about the details. Max rips open two boxes of tiles and holds up a sheet of each one to the kitchen backsplash, then turns to me.

"What do you think?"

I stand back to consider both options. "The right one."

"Cool," he says, putting the left sheet back into its box.

My phone rings from my bedroom, which makes my smart watch go off. "It's already past noon?" I grumble, letting out a sigh. "I have three video conferences today, so I'm going to close my door to muffle all the tool sounds. If you need me," I say, stopping mid-sentence and shrugging. "Actually, don't need me. I'll be busy all day. Work stuff."

"No problem. I'll be quiet."

I head back toward my room, stopping when Max calls my name.

"You want pizza for dinner? I can get some delivered."

I look at him for exactly half a second before averting my gaze. *Piece of furniture.*

"Sure," I say, because saying "Heck no, leave me alone, I'm trying to be independent" would just be rude.

Plus I love pizza.

Chapter Four

My best friend Annie makes gaga eyes at me on our video chat, her thick dark eyebrows going up and down suggestively. "He must be really hot."

I roll my eyes. I've only told her the briefest of information about my unwanted, unexpected roommate Max. The timer on my phone says we've been talking thirty seven seconds. That's not nearly long enough for her to gather that he's totally hot, but she's right. He is.

"He's just some guy." I keep my voice low, a slight bit above a whisper. It's just after seven in the morning here in Texas, which means it's eight in New Jersey where Annie lives. She just got off a night shift at the hospital so we catch up in the mornings before she falls asleep for the day.

"What does he look like?" She wiggles her eyebrows again.

"He looks like a guy who better hurry up and finish the remodel so he can leave."

"Why are you whispering?"

"So he doesn't hear me!"

Annie tosses her head back in a laugh. "You're the biggest dork, Jules, but I love you."

I heave a sigh. "This is just really bad timing. I'm supposed to be working on my next novel and I'm already behind schedule. I had planned on diving into writing the second I unpacked and now most of my crap is in the hallway waiting on Mr. Fix-it to finish!"

"When is the manuscript due to your editor?" she asks, using her phone screen as a mirror to check her hair.

"In two months."

"That's not too bad. How much do you have written?"

I bite my lip. "None of it."

"What!"

I jump, lowering the volume on my phone. "It's just been so hard lately. Between the breakup and the move and stifling the urge to eat five gallons of ice cream each day, it's just been hard to get started on my next book. I was supposed to move in yesterday and then immediately write and now..." I crinkle up my face and glance toward my closed bedroom door. On the other side of it is my dream home in a mid-renovation mess.

I sigh. "I'm too stressed to write."

Annie frowns. "What happens if you don't meet the deadline?"

This is the question I've been avoiding for weeks now. Pushing it to the back of my mind and pretending it won't ever happen. I had hoped—no, I had *known*—that once I moved into this gorgeous house on the lake I'd be fully rested, motivated, and inspired to write my next book. And now... that's not going according to plan.

"I don't know..." I say softly as dread builds in my stomach. "My publisher already paid me a huge advance, which I spent on this house. I can't think about missing the deadline because it can't happen. I have to write this book."

"Well get to it, girl!" Annie smiles, flashing me her bright white teeth. My beautiful Filipina best friend is just as stunning even after pulling a twelve hour overnight shift. "You can do it. Get off the phone and go write."

I still have a ton of things to do, like go grocery shopping, buy a new coffee maker to replace mine that broke in the move, and order a bed frame. But the weight of this deadline is hanging over my head, so even though it's super early in the morning, I decide to get some writing done before I go run errands, that way I can start my day off on the right foot. Maybe getting a few chapters written will help crush the weight of this deadline that's been heavy on my shoulders.

I sit on my squishy new mattress, laptop in front of me. I open a blank document and place my hands on the keyboard. *You can do this*, I think. *Don't stress about life. Just get to work.*

The jarring sound of a power tool rips through the air the second my hands land on the keyboard. My eyes widen. Seriously?

I type: Chapter One.

The sound continues.

In a huff, I close my laptop, crawl off my on-the-floor mattress and step out into the chaos of the renovations. A large blue tarp is spread out on the kitchen floor. The windows are open, the back door has been propped open with a brick, and Max the handyman stands on the back porch doing some weird thing with a drill and a bucket.

"Good morning," I say, hands on my hips as I stand just inside the house watching him. The bucket has a chalky substance, and I can see now that his power drill is attached to some kind of metal mixing wand that's stirring the stuff in the bucket. It's like a cake mixer but for construction.

"Good morning," Max says over the whirring of his drill. He glances over and flashes me a bright welcoming smile.

"I was being sarcastic."

"Huh?" he calls out over the noise.

"I was being sarcastic!" I yell back—only he shuts off the drill in the middle of my sentence so I end up yelling the last word.

His lips quirk into a smile. "Sarcasm this early in the morning?"

"I'm trying to work, and this..." I gesture toward the junk on the back porch. A bucket, boxes of tile and other things that belong on a construction job site. "It's really loud."

Will I ever get my dream house all to myself? This looks like it'll take forever.

"Sorry," he says, wiping his brow with the back of a gloved hand. "I'm almost finished mixing the grout, then it'll be quieter while I tile the kitchen."

"Great!" I turn around and go back to my bedroom.

And then the music starts.

I stand in the hallway watching him for at least a full minute and he doesn't even notice. Max is dancing. He's *actually* dancing around my kitchen, his feet shuffling and his head bopping to the music while he scoops out grout from the bucket and scrapes it across the kitchen backsplash.

I walk over and wave my hand to get his attention. He grins, nodding his head at me.

"Are you seriously dancing right now?"

"You only get one life," he says, grabbing my hand. Before I know what's happening, he spins me around on the plastic-covered kitchen floor. "Why not make it fun?"

He lets me go after one spin and I put my hands on my hips. "What are you, two?"

"I'm almost thirty," he says, swaying his head from left to right. Now that I'm watching him, he's getting all groovy with the music, even more than before. "Let me guess... you're in your late twenties but you have the personality of an eighty-year old school marm."

"You think you're funny but you're not."

He grins. "I don't think I'm funny."

I can sense his stupid punchline before he says it.

"I know I'm funny."

Yep. There it is. I roll my eyes so epically that

they're in danger of getting stuck in the back of my head. I reach over and turn off the Bluetooth speaker.

"I have to work. You want to listen to music? Get headphones."

"Aww, that's no fun," he says. "Headphones get sweaty."

"Ew," I say, looking a little more repulsed than I actually feel. "How much longer are these renovations supposed to take?"

"A few weeks," he says to the wall as he slides the grout across it, his metal tool leaving perfect grooves in it. "Three, maybe four."

"Oh heck no. That is way too long."

"I can only work as fast as I can work."

I heave a sigh and look around at the mess. My deadline will be here before I know it and if this guy is going to be jamming music and using power tools every day for three to four weeks, I'll never get a single word written.

Then I get an idea. A spark, an inspiration. Something I haven't had with my writing, but at least it's inspiration for something else that matters. "What if I helped?"

He lowers his grouting tool and turns around. There's a small smudge of dirt or grout or something on his forehead, but he's still so handsome it takes my breath away.

"You want to help renovate?

I shrug. "Anything to get some peace and quiet around here."

"Okay," he says flashing me that bright smile of his. "Hope you have some paint clothes."

Chapter Five

I do not, in fact, have paint clothes. As part of my downsizing and moving across the state plan, I had tossed anything that wasn't in excellent condition, leaving my wardrobe made up of all my nice things. But that won't stop me from helping with this renovation and getting Max's stupid butt out of my house as soon as possible. I shake my head.

Do not think about his butt.

My phone's GPS guides me to the nearest thrift store so I can find an old T-shirt and leggings that can be my official paint clothes. My bedroom is the only room that's fully painted, and everywhere else in the house has only been primed. That's a lot of walls and not much time to paint them.

After going on a three-for-a-dollar T-shirt spree at

the thrift store, my stomach grumbles loudly reminding me that I haven't eaten anything since Max's pizza last night. The only grocery store in Sterling is small but charming. I pop in and browse around for some groceries, loading up on orange soda, sour candies, and popcorn—my three most essential writing snacks, as well as some other essentials, like ice cream, frozen tater tots, and various junk foods. Sometimes I'm only an adult in age, not personality. But if I'm going to get anything written, I need my writer fuel: sugar.

Back at home, Max's music blares through the speakers, but he turns it down when he sees me walk in the front door. The kitchen backsplash looks great. He managed to get the whole thing tiled in the couple of hours I've been gone.

"What's that?" Max asks, brows pulling together as I lug in my grocery bags. I resist rolling my eyes and snapping that a real man would offer to help a lady carry groceries. Men suck, and I already know that. No point in saying anything about it. Besides, even if he had offered to help, I'd still turn him down. I can do this on my own.

"It's food," I say, hefting the bag onto the counter.

"Oh, no." Max sucks in air through his teeth. "Did Kelly not tell you that we have no appliances?"

My eyes widen. Sure enough, there's a gaping hole in the kitchen cabinets where the refrigerator should be. And another space for a dishwasher and oven. Above the oven space is yet another empty space where a microwave should be mounted. I stare at the tall rectangular fridge space and wonder when exactly I fell and hit my head and became someone who doesn't notice when *very large appliances* are missing!

"Did you get anything cold?" Max asks, scratching the back of his neck.

I toss my head back and groan. "Yes, I did. Because I'm an idiot. And I'm so freaking hungry I was really looking forward to cooking something for lunch."

"Ah, Julie, I'm sorry. Good news is that new appliances will be delivered in three days. Kelly said they were all stainless steel, so they'll look great."

I huff out another sigh before thinking of an idea that might, maybe, possibly work, assuming that small town folks are as sweet and charming as they're often portrayed in the movies. I do a quick reshuffle of my bags, putting the frozen and cold stuff into three bags. Then I walk down the street to the blouse with the white door. What was her name? Lina?

Lina welcomes me into her house, and after I explain my problem, she's happy to let me store my stuff in her fridge until mine arrives in a few days. I'll take that as a win. Small towns really are as great as they seem.

Back at home, Max has put away his grouting supplies. The rushing water coming from the bathroom tells me he's taking a shower. It's a quick shower, because I've barely even put the rest of my groceries into the cabinets when he emerges. Instantly, my brain conjures up an image of Max wearing a towel around his waist, beads of water covering his muscled torso. He walks out fully dressed in jeans and a red t-shirt, hair slightly damp in waves across his forehead.

Bummer.

I mean, not bummer. I don't care one bit.

"There's a great diner not too far from here," he says, running a towel across his hair. "Wanna get some lunch before we get back to work?"

How is it that a man can shower and look so put together in just fifteen minutes? So not fair, Mother Nature. You did us women dirty.

"Sure," I say, surprised my starving monster of a stomach didn't growl out the word for me.

Roger's diner should have a much cooler name because the place is incredible. It's right on the water, just half a mile away from my house, with outdoor seating on the decking that overlooks Lake Sterling. The menu has everything you could want, from breakfast to burgers to milkshakes and more. My mouth waters just looking through the laminated pages of delicious food. The prices are also cheaper than anything I've seen in Dallas. Ah, small town life. You're the best.

Max sits across from me, quiet as we both read our menus. Sure, it's a little awkward sitting here with a man in a totally platonic way, especially when I'm sharing a house with him, but at the moment I am too hungry to care.

Even our waitress is straight out of a small town cliché. She's mid-40's with her blonde hair piled high in a gorgeous messy bun on top of her head. Her bright red lipstick makes me smile. The waitresses back where I'm from are overworked, overstressed college students who couldn't be bothered to tell you good morning.

"Welcome, welcome," she sing-songs as she drops off our drink orders. I got a Dr. Pepper and Max ordered an unsweet tea. Gross. Who doesn't like sugar in everything at every given time? Finally, I'm seeing a flaw in Max, who otherwise seems like a pretty decent guy. I order a cheeseburger and fries. Max orders a BLT with a side salad.

"Ew," I say after our waitress is out of earshot. "A side salad?"

Max quirks an eyebrow. "They have good salads here."

My grimace intensifies. "Your BLT has lettuce and tomato on it. That's basically a salad on a sandwich so getting a side salad is redundant."

He snorts. "I like salads."

"Cheese fries are better."

Deep down, I like salads too. I mean, not all the time and not as a side when you could have fries, but they're okay. I can't help myself, though. Whatever Max likes I am determined to not like. It might be childish, but it reminds me of my promise to myself. No more romance. No more hot guys or flirty chitchat. The old Julie would have happily pretended to love everything a guy loved just so they'd like me. Not anymore.

Our waitress brings out a pitcher of water to refill his cup.

"Good to see you're dating again," she says, turning to me with a wink. "Honey, he's a keeper, I promise."

I choke on my cheeseburger, then rush to take a sip of my soda to cover my coughing. My cheeks turn red.

"Not a date," Max says, glancing up at the waitress. He cuts me some slack by not even looking over at how embarrassing I look right now. "She's new to town. And just a friend."

"Oh," she says, frowning as if this is the worst news she's heard all day. "Welcome to Sterling, hun. What's your name?"

"I'm Julie."

"Hi, Julie." She puts a hand on my shoulder and leans down. I guess she thinks she's being subtle, but her voice is not quiet at all when she whispers, "Max is a good man. A real, real, good man."

Max's hand covers his face. I wait until she's gone before snorting out a laugh. "That wasn't awkward or anything."

"Yeah, sorry about her. She's been friends with my mom forever. She's probably off calling her right now because in her mind, there's no way a guy can just be friends with a woman."

I shrug. "Joke is on her because I don't date."

"Never?" He stabs his fork into his salad. "Or not anymore?"

"Never again," I say. A weird silence falls over us and I don't know what gets into me but I'm compelled to keep talking. Stupid soda sugar rush. "There was a time in my life where I was stupid enough to think romance was real. Now I'm older and wiser and know better."

"Maybe I'm dumb, but I've still got hope."

I snort. "Have fun getting disappointed."

That weird silence falls over us again, so I concentrate on dunking my fries into ketchup. Even with the sound of the breeze rustling through the trees, and the children laughing a few tables over, it just feels very, very quiet in the space between Max and me.

"So what do you do for a living?" Max asks. He must feel it too.

"I'm a writer."

"Journalism and stuff?"

I shake my head over a mouthful of buttery roll. "Novels."

He nods, impressed. "Wow. That's awesome. What kind of books do you write?"

I take another bite. The great thing about being single forever is that you don't have to worry about looking like a gross slob who talks with their mouth full. "I write about a private investigator who tracks down cheating bastards and makes them pay."

His eyebrow quirks. "I guess you won't be writing the next great romance novel any time soon?"

I snort. "Never in a million years. Romance is stupid."

Chapter Six

By the time we're home from lunch I'm struggling with my brain to figure out how I feel about this whole thing. I'm still just as in love with my new house as ever, especially the stunning back porch that faces the water, so that's not a problem at all. This whole Max thing is the problem.

Because he's kind of awesome?

Like, just as a friend, of course.

I want to hate him, but he's funny and kind and he eats salads like some kind of weirdo who cares about his health. All these good qualities are starting to topple over the wall of hatred I'd built up in my heart, the wall that tells me I hate men and I won't ever be friends with them.

Maybe that's a little too harsh. Just because I hate

romance doesn't mean I have to hate men. Just because Max is incredibly hot doesn't mean I should hate him, too. I mean, good for him. Good for his genetics and his working out habits that give him those muscles, and good on the sun for making his skin all tanned and gorgeous and GOOD FOR HIM. He's handsome. Good for him.

I take a deep breath.

"You okay?"

Max's sudden voice startles me from my thoughts. We're home now, walking into the living room, and I barely even noticed it. I nod. "Yep. Time to paint."

"Cool," he says. "I'll go install the new outdoor light fixtures."

My chest constricts a bit once he leaves. I don't know why his mere presence does things to my insides, like wake up butterflies that have been dormant for months. It's really annoying. Too bad these butterflies can't help write my manuscript.

I shrug it off and stare at the paint supplies on the floor in front of me. I've never actually painted any walls before, but I've seen enough Home Depot commercials to know you dunk the roller thingy in the paint and then slather it over the wall. Should be easy enough.

It is not easy.

I barely managed to pour a heavy gallon of paint into the metal tray thingy without spilling or dumping it everywhere. Then the paint gooped down the side of the can, making a mess of everything because in a split second, I decided to stop the paint spillage with my hands, and now I'm standing in the middle of my living room, grateful as heck for the drop cloth on the floor because my hands are covered in super thick paint. It doesn't scrape off into the bucket very easily. The kitchen and bathroom sinks are brand new, the faucets still shiny and nice. I can't touch them to wash off my hands.

There has to be a water hose outside, right? Worst case scenario, I'll wash my hands in the lake. With an elbow maneuver that probably makes me look like a T-Rex, I manage to open the back door without getting paint on anything except my own clothing, my hair, my cheek, and my dignity. Outside, I wander around the porch looking for a water faucet, a garden hose, anything.

I walk around the house and find a spigot. Yes!

"You okay there?"

"I'm great. Just washing my hands," I say, not looking up from the task at hand. Light blue paint splashes onto the grass beneath the water stream.

"Wow, you've already taped everything up? You

work fast."

I turn off the water and glance up at Max, who is all lean muscle beneath his grease-stained work shirt.

"Tape?"

His brow furrows as he follows me back inside. He surveys the floor, which has a tray of paint, a paint-covered gallon bucket, and very clean untouched paint rollers.

"Have you never painted before?"

"I'm a city girl," I say, which should tell him all he needs to know. Judging by the curious look on his face, it doesn't. "I've always lived in condos and you're not allowed to paint rental homes."

"You have to tape first," he says, bending to grab a roll of blue masking tape. "All the corners and edges around the windows and ceiling. You know, so you don't get paint on the parts that don't need paint?"

"Ah," I say with a slow nod. "That would make a lot of sense."

He smiles, that genuine, adorable Max smile I've come to know in just two days. It's not sarcastic like how Jason used to make fun of me, and it's not slimy like a frat boy. It's just a smile. It's kind of sweet.

"I'll tape, you paint?" he suggests.

"Sure," I say.

He peels off a strip of tape and expertly applies it

around the white window trim. I watch him work, admiring his strong arms as they place tape all around it and then move onto the next one. I should probably start painting, but, I'm mesmerized by his skill.

He turns around to face me and I jump, then reach for the bag of foam paint rollers to make it look like I'm doing something.

"Hey, Julie?"

"Hmm?"

"Would you hate me right now if I suggested playing some music?"

"Music would be great." It'll drown out the sound of my pounding heart and hopefully cover up all this awkwardness I have. Why am I so awkward? I should totally be freaking out about how I'm behind on my writing, but instead I'm just kind of... enjoying the moment?

Weird. This is so weird.

"What kind of music do you like?" he asks.

"Anything," I say.

He plays Weezer through the Bluetooth speaker and I grin. "Nice choice," I say, bobbing my head along to the words for All My Favorite Songs, one of the band's best works if you ask me.

We slip into a nice routine. He tapes up a wall and then we both work to paint it. He's taller, so he uses the roller to get the high spots on the wall, and I kneel on the floor with a handheld paintbrush to paint the boarder of the room. The music keeps us company. Before long, we've finished the entire living room and Max suggests we do the small study next.

The study is half the size of my bedroom and it has no closet. A twin sized air mattress is on the floor. He has a duffel bag of clothing, a cell phone plugged into the charger, and a laptop.

"You travel light," I say as he takes all his stuff and moves it to the center of the room so we can paint.

"Yeah, I don't need much."

It suddenly occurs to me that I'm taking Max's home two months earlier than he had planned on moving.

"Where will you live after my house is done?"

"I'll just go home," he says, ripping off the blue tape with his teeth. I try not to stare at his lips in the process.

Home? Ew. This guy lives with his parents? He's almost thirty!

I know I shouldn't judge people, especially in this economy, but nothing pushes me away quite like a man without his own place to live. It's always the guys who live at home who screw me over. They either have no money and they wanted to move in with me, which

I refuse, or they have weirdly strict parents who won't let "girls" over to visit even though I'm a woman and we're both adults. One of the reasons I liked Jason was because he had his own place in my same complex. He was independent. Too bad that's not the only quality that makes a guy boyfriend material.

"You do have a nice mom," I say.

"Huh?" He snorts. "I didn't mean my parents' home. I meant my house."

"You have a house?"

He nods, moving closer to tape the ceiling above me. My stomach flutters at our nearness. I take a step back.

"My brother lost his job so he and his family were going to be homeless a few months ago," he explains. "He's got a wife and two little kids so told them to move into my place until he's back on his feet. I can just crash on the couch."

"Oh," I say, feeling breathless. "Cool."

He's got his own house? He gave it up for his family?

He's gorgeous and handy and thoughtful *and* he eats salads?

Oh gosh. Oh no.

My heart is developing a crush.

And my brain seems powerless to stop it.

Chapter Seven

My entire body hurts by the time we've finished painting. Like, every single muscle is screaming in agony right now. My body is a writer's body. I'm meant to sit in a comfy chair, only exercising my fingers while I type out my next bestseller. I am not built for six hours of painting.

Max takes the paint stuff outside to rinse it off, and I'm supposed to go shower, but I'm just laying here on the floor of my bedroom, staring at the ceiling with zero willpower to get back up again.

There's a soft tap on my door, followed by, "You hungry? We can head to the diner for dinner."

"That sounds amazing," I say, lolling my head to the side to look at him. "I need to shower first."

"I thought you were doing that thirty minutes ago?"

I sit up. "It's been *thirty minutes?*"

He chuckles. "Have you been laying there the whole time?"

I drag a tired hand across my face. "I guess I have."

"Mind if I shower first?"

I nod, laying back down on the cool hardwood flooring. "Be my guest."

"Cool," he says, tapping on the doorframe. "I'll shower then finish something on the back porch real quick, then I'm ready whenever you are."

"What's broken on the back porch?" I ask, staring at the ceiling. The back porch looked fine last time I was out there.

"It's a surprise."

"Fine," I say with a yawn. "Keep your secrets."

There must have been something in my Diet Coke at the dinner. Alcohol? Magic fairy dust? Something. Because it's like the normal Julie has been yanked out of my body and replaced with a cooler, more fun, flirtatious Julie. Max and I had so much fun at Roger's Diner. He'd introduced me to a few of the locals, and when our neighbor Lina showed up with her husband, we'd pushed our tables together and had dinner with them.

Everyone loves Max. He's so kind, and friendly, and sweet.

I find myself sneaking glances at him during the short drive back home. Here in the cab of his truck, I can smell his cologne. It's cool and soft, reminding me of the ocean. I know I have to get back to writing my manuscript. I know he needs to finish renovating my house and get out of here so my life can truly start over here in Sterling. All of that needs to happen ASAP.

But for now... I really like this.

"Ready for your surprise?" Max asks after parking next to my Jeep in the driveway.

"Surprise?"

"The porch," he says with a mischievous grin.

"Sure." I know I'm smiling back, but I try to keep my voice calm and natural.

We make our way through the house which now smells like fresh paint and looks clean and open with all the paint supplies gone. As I step out onto the porch, I don't notice anything different.

"Well?" I say, turning around to cock my head at Max, who promised a surprise. "I don't see anything different."

"How about now?"

He flips a light switch by the back door. The dark summery sky lights up. My jaw drops as I look up. The wide back porch has a pergola roof, thin wooden slats that provide some shade during the day. Max has strung up a crisscrossed pattern of clear outdoor lights. Out on the lake, the water seems to sparkle and glow even prettier now. I turn in a slow circle, taking in the magical glow of the lights mixed with the soft sounds of nature and the crisp smell of clean, country air.

"You're incredible," I say, my voice a soft whisper as I peer up at this man who feels so much more important than he was a day ago.

"That's not all," Max says. A little dimple forms in his cheek when he smirks. He holds up a remote control. "LED lights. They change colors."

I watch as the lights overhead change from clear to blue, green, purple, pink.

"Leave it pink!" I say, basking in the soft glow of my favorite color. "It's like a nightclub but without all the stupid people and lame music."

"Should I leave?" Max jokes. "That way there's no stupid people here?"

I roll my eyes, taking a step closer and pressing my hands to his chest. "You're not stupid so you can stay."

"Really?" he murmurs. I'm keenly aware of his

hands lightly wrapping around me. "I thought you couldn't stand me."

I shrug. "I feel differently now." My hands slide up his chest and settle on his shoulders. They have a mind of their own, these hands. Funny little things.

Seriously, what was in my Diet Coke?

I don't know exactly how it happens. I swear I don't. And if you ask me later, I will deny, deny, deny.

But it happens. I am kissing Max.

He leans down and I lift up and we hold each other, softly but surely, as our lips touch. I breathe in the smell of that cologne, taste the Dr. Pepper on his lips. His soft, perfect lips. Every single thought in my head disappears and the only thing that matters is this moment, kissing this gorgeous man under the pink glow of my porch lights, secretly hoping this moment will never end.

My best friend Annie changed my ringtone the day after Jason and I broke up. I had been a crying, blubbering mess. I was so upset I'd done the hardest thing a writer can do— deleted the romantic manuscript I was working on. It just didn't feel right to keep writing about two fictional lovebirds in a fictionally happy relationship when I knew I was writing lies. In that moment, I'd felt like my career was over. That I'd never be able to write romance again, and I'd never sell another book, and my fans would dump me and I'd be the biggest loser ever.

Luckily, I found a new way to revive my career by writing anti-romance books. But before that fantastic idea, I was a mess. Annie did everything she could to cheer me up. She brought ice cream, pizza, candy, and even cleaned my condo for me from top to bottom. The ringtone thing was a joke. I usually keep my phone on silent, but tonight I'd turned the ringer on since my phone stayed in my room while I painted all day and I wanted to hear it.

So it's right about now, when my toes are tingly and my body is melting to goo and my lips still feel warm from the kiss—*the kiss!!*—when Fate decides to smack me back to reality before this moment goes too far.

He rocks in the tree tops all day long
Hoppin' and a-boppin' and a-singing his song
"What's that?" Max asks.

"It's my phone." I roll my eyes as the cheerful music of Bobby Day's famous song plays loudly through the house. Max's arms slide away from my waist.

Rockin' robin tweet tweet tweet
Rockin' robin tweet, tweedle-lee-dee
"Do you need to answer that?"

I shake my head, biting my lip as waves of regret wash over me. "They'll leave a message."

"Cool." He grins, leaning forward. "Where were we?"

My arms are around his neck before I know it, and my toes are lifting me up off the porch before I know it, and my lips—those freaking traitors—are on his lips before I know it.

It only takes half a second to fall back into this blissful moment, lit up by the glow of porch lights and framed by the beautiful midnight blue of the late-evening sky.

He rocks in the tree tops all day long
Hoppin' and a-boppin' and a-singing his song
Like a bucket of cold water hitting me in the face, my phone rings again, ruining the moment, yet again.

"Ugh."

I step backward, mentally shaking myself off.

"You should go answer that," Max says. "Could be important."

"Right," I say, sucking in air through my teeth as I turn and rush into the house. My agent's name lights up my phone screen. Oh wow. It really is important.

"Hello?" I answer, barely able to hear my own voice over the rush of my beating heart.

"Julie, I have fantastic news," she says. "Sorry to

call late, but it's a big deal. Clark TV wants to interview you about your new book series!"

"Oh, wow!" I lean against the wall in my bedroom for support. "Seriously?"

Clark TV is the biggest entertainment channel. They have the number one entertainment podcast and cable show. This is big. This is huge.

"Yep. They're sending a camera crew out and you'll be interviewed by Zoey herself!"

"Sending a camera crew where?" I ask.

"To your address! How cool is that? You don't even have to go anywhere."

"Oh..."

"Make sure you play up the single thing," my agent cheerfully drones on. "They love how you went from romantic to fierce single woman."

Yep. Fierce single woman.

That's me.

Chapter Eight

"I'm gonna throw up." I grab my stomach and lean against the kitchen counter. It's been five minutes since the call with my agent and I'm in full panic attack mode. The delicious Monte Cristo sandwich I had at the diner threatens to come right back up, and I have a suspicion it won't be so delicious this time around. I grit my teeth and try to breathe, but it feels like hyperventilating instead of breathing.

Max's hand touches my back. "Julie?"

"I'm fine," I squeak out, pushing away from him and scurrying to my room. I fall on my bed and drag in air through my teeth. The nausea isn't real—I'm not truly sick, but anxious and panicky and—

Holy crap did I kiss Max?

I roll onto my back and cover my hands with my face. My cheeks are hot. My heart is pounding. I lay like this for a long time, or maybe no time at all. How am I supposed to know? I'm too busy freaking out!

The next thing I know I'm waking up to the morning sunlight filtering in through my window. I'm still wearing the clothes I wore to dinner last night, which means my face is also sporting day-old makeup. Ew. My bladder screams at me to go pee, but peeing means leaving my room and leaving my room means facing Max and facing Max means remembering how I kissed him.

And I shouldn't be kissing anybody. Not anymore, and never again.

I am an independent woman who does not make her money on romance novels anymore.

Oh gosh, my bladder does not care about my personal problems. Unless I want to completely humiliate myself by having some kind of accident like a toddler, I have to get up and face the music.

On my tiptoes, I prance my way to the door. This house is so new to me that I haven't memorized which floorboards are squeaky and which will let me sneak around unnoticed. I make it to the hallway, and around my boxes of junk, without making a sound. I can't hear Max's tools or music, so hopefully he's still asleep.

Once I'm in the bathroom, I pee like I've never peed in my entire life, and then I try to figure out where I go from here. I could cancel the TV interview, but that would be the dumbest career choice I've ever made. You can't just turn down Clark TV.

I wash my hands and then brush my teeth. I really need a shower, but I'm too frazzled for that much hygiene so early in the morning. The only thing that would be more draining than a shower right now would be talking to Max.

I dry my hands on the bathroom towel and then open the door.

"Morning!"

Max sits on a lawn chair in the living room, a mug of coffee in one hand and an iPad in the other. He wears black sweatpants that look sexier than any pair of sweatpants should be allowed to look, and a gray T-shirt that hugs tightly to his well-defined chest. The man is a dreamboat even when he's slummin' it.

"You want some coffee?"

"Yes."

I don't even look at him as I walk past him to the kitchen where I pour myself a cup of blonde roast. Not looking only does so much. He's still here. Still just a few feet away, looking like what the teenagers call *a snack.*

I tell myself not to get all loopy and drooly and heart-eye-emoji around him. But it doesn't matter what my brain tells my heart—they are two fundamentally different organs and my heart seems to win out every single time. Throw me into a burning building and my brain will take over, knowing I should crawl down low, cover my mouth with a wet cloth to avoid breathing in toxic fumes, and get out as fast as possible.

But put me in a room with Max Spenser? I'm a goner, apparently. Too swoony-eyed and butterfly-stomached to function as a rational human being. My brain knows how to save me. My heart, well, I think that thing is working against me. It's out to get me. It wants me to suffer.

Ugh, I'm so disgusted in myself I could scream. Maybe I should scream. Maybe screaming would help.

"You okay?" Max asks. "Looks like your mind is running on overdrive."

I shrug and try to put on a passive, apathetic expression while I stir powdered creamer into my coffee. "I'm fine."

"I think you're lying."

I look up at him. He offers me that soft, comforting smile of his. His smile always has a way of breaking through my hardened exterior. I feel myself melt a bit. Then I shrug it off and remember the problem at hand.

"So, here's the thing," I say. If I treat him like the guy who is remodeling my house instead of the guy I kissed last night, maybe I can solve two problems. "I'm going to be interviewed for Clark TV. They want to come to my house to set up their cameras and cushy chairs and stuff so Zoey can interview me."

"Wow, that's awesome," Max says, his face lighting up. "I had no idea you were so famous."

I shrug. "I'm not. Well... not before now. This is a big deal, and it's a life changer for my career and," I toss my hands up gesturing to the mess around us. "My house isn't ready."

"When is the interview?"

"Four days."

Determination sharpens his features. He nods. "We can do it all in four days."

"Really?"

"Yeah. If we get to work now, we'll be good. Appliances are almost here. I can take all the construction trash to the dumpster. There's not much left."

"That would be awesome," I say, looking around

and trying to visualize my house being done and shiny and perfect.

He stands, chugging the rest of his coffee in one gulp. I try to look away from his bicep, from the angle of his jaw, the coffee mug pressed to his lips.

"Let's get to work."

Chapter Nine

The appliances arrive the next day and Max helps the delivery guy hook them up in the kitchen. They look amazing, and even better—now I can put my cold food somewhere besides my neighbor's house. Every time I swing by to get something from her fridge, she makes a comment about Max, as if she can't understand why I'm not falling madly in love with him. I guess I have a good poker face.

The last of the paint touchups are done, thanks to my newfound skills as a painter. I may have suddenly forgotten how to write, but I can paint. We get all the light figures replaced with modern, sleek new designs, and the light switch and electrical outlet covers get replaced with crisp new ones. Max and I hang curtain rods and nail the address number onto the front of the house, just under the porch. We get everything cleaned up and Max even takes me to the furniture store and lets me use his truck to haul a new couch and some bedroom furniture. We get a cute kitchen table and chairs from a local thrift shop.

Max and I are up at six in the morning every day, working constantly, only taking a break for lunch and dinner, which we get at the diner. Everything comes together so quickly. My hallway boxes are easy to unpack once all the renovation clutter is gone. In just three short days, the house is ready. *My* house is ready. It's even more beautiful than I imagined.

My new gray couch is as comfortable as it is beautiful. My artwork on the walls is a mixture of new stuff I found in town and the old stuff I brought with me. Max has been a huge help by driving me everywhere and letting me use the bed of his truck to haul all my new stuff. I've blown through pretty much all of the huge book advance I got for my new series, but it'll be worth it if I look amazing in my TV interview.

To celebrate the house being done and the kitchen being functional, I cook us dinner on the third night after we've finished everything. It's just a simple lasagna made from the recipe they print on the box of noodles, but Max can't stop complimenting it.

"This is really good," he says, his mouth full. He's

on his third piece of lasagna and he's devoured half of the garlic bread. I wish I could eat like a man and stay as sexy as he is. If I were to say that out loud, he'd probably mention all those salads he also eats to balance out his diet. So I don't say it out loud. I'm a junk food fiend for life, baby.

I shake the thought from my mind. Max is not allowed to be sexy. I can't think that. I certainly can't let my mind drift back toward that night when we kissed under the incredibly romantic lights he installed on my porch. The best part of staying so busy the last few days was that it gave me very little time to think about things I shouldn't think about.

The worst part is that it's been another three days and I haven't written a single word for my new manuscript. I set my fork down, suddenly no longer hungry now that my stomach is in knots of anxiety. There is still so much work to do. How am I supposed to sit through my interview with Zoey and pretend I'm a professional author when I haven't even started my new book yet?

"Thanks again for dinner," Max says, reaching for another piece of garlic bread. "It's been a long time since someone has made me a meal."

"You deserve, like, five hundred homecooked meals for all the help you've been," I say, forcing a smile while my mind is still worrying about my interview tomorrow.

"Nah," he says, standing up and taking our plates to the sink. To my surprise, he starts washing them. I want to tell him not to worry about it, that it's my house and my dishes and I'll wash them but the sight of him standing there, all muscular and tanned skin from doing construction work, putting his talents to use in the kitchen is just so incredibly sexy.

My brain kicks on, my imaginary personification of it stands tall and pushes my heart out of the way. My brain works on overtime, trying so hard to tell my heart what it needs to hear: that crushing on Max will only lead to trouble.

"I can get out of here tonight," Max says, after drying and putting away the dishes.

"Huh?" I'm so stuck in my own thoughts, I was only half paying attention and I'm not sure what he just said.

"I'll leave tonight," he clarifies, drying his hands on a dish towel. "With the renovations done, it's all your house now."

"Don't be silly." I wave my hand toward him. "It's almost dark outside. You can stay tonight."

"You sure?"

As sure as I want to kiss you again.

I keep my thoughts to myself and just nod.

"Max?"

It's not until two seconds after I knock on his door that I realize what this looks like. It's one in the morning, and I'm waking him up. Typically, that means one thing.

Typically, it doesn't mean a panic attack.

"Julie?" His voice is groggy from sleep. "Come in."

I probably shouldn't go into his room, but I can't stop pacing. My heart races. I need to talk to someone. Annie didn't answer her phone this late at night, and I need to talk.

"I'm freaking out," I say after lightly pushing open the door.

He sits up on his air mattress. He's shirtless, and that's not even phasing me right now, which is a testament to how much I'm freaking out.

"I'm freaking out," I say again while his eyes blink awake.

He stands, turning on the light. Concern darkens his features. "What's wrong?"

My breathing is shallow. It feels like I've been running a marathon when all I've done for the last few hours is lay awake in bed. I open my mouth to talk but the words stick in my throat.

Finally, I think of something to say.

"Could you maybe put a shirt on?"

He smirks. "Sure."

"Sorry," I say, feeling the tension in my shoulders ease up just a bit. "It's just..." I wave my hand in front of his chest. "Distracting."

He smirks again. My knees get weak.

Then another wave of anxiety hits me and I remember why I'm in the middle of a panic attack.

"So what's up?" he says, guiding me to the living room and sitting next to me on the couch.

"I'm freaking out."

"I can tell," he says, his gentle smile making my heart flutter.

I run my hands through my hair. "The interview tomorrow... I can't do it."

"Yes, you can. You'll be great."

I shake my head. "No, I won't. I'll look like an idiot!"

"They chose you for a reason. They want you. That means you're already qualified for it."

I look down at my lap. "Maybe the old me would have been good, but not right now. I don't even feel like a real author right now."

"Why?"

I shrug. "I haven't written in weeks. I'm supposed to be halfway finished with my new manuscript by now and I don't have any of it done. I'm a failure. I had success with a new book and now everyone expects more from me and I don't know if I can do it. I don't know if I can write the books they want me to write."

"I'm sorry," he says. He reaches up and puts a hand on my shoulder. "I don't know anything about being a writer, but it sounds hard. What kind of book do they want you to write?"

My breath shudders. I should just tell him the truth. That I write about Rosa Ramirez, the anti-romance private investigator who takes down crappy men one at a time. I should tell him how much I hate romance. Hate relationships. How much I refuse to ever be caught in one again.

But my words stick in my throat and all I do is shrug. "It doesn't matter," I say. "I just need to find a way to get through this interview without looking like a total loser."

"No one will think you're a loser," he says, squeezing my shoulder. "You're amazing."

All those same magical feelings from the night on the porch come back, manifesting themselves in the space between us on the couch. The hair on my neck prickles to life. My lips get all fuzzy and warm and desperate to kiss him. He looks impossibly handsome from the glow of the lamp in the corner of the room. His dirty blond hair is messy and practically begging me to run my hands through it.

I swallow.

"Can we talk?" he says quietly, his eyes telling me everything I need to know.

I shake my head. "I'd rather not."

He frowns. "You know what I want to talk about?"

I nod quickly.

"The thing we haven't talked about?"

I nod again. "I can't talk about it."

He chews his bottom lip and then looks up at me. "We kissed, Julie. We kissed. And it was nice. Really nice."

A deep blush creeps up my cheeks.

Max's cheeks look a little flushed too. "I was hoping to do it again."

"I'm sorry," I say. My voice sounds so far away. Like it belongs to someone else. Some other idiot who is about to turn down this gorgeous, incredible guy. I swallow. "That kiss was a mistake."

"Was it? It didn't feel like a mistake."

"It was."

"Okay. Well, thanks for clarifying."

"Max, I don't mean to hurt you it's just…"

He shakes his head. "No worries, Julie. It's fine. I'll be out of your hair in the morning."

He walks to his room and closes the door.

I want so badly to run to him, to tell him that the kiss did mean something. That it felt more real than anything with any man has felt in my life. But I hold back.

It's the right thing to do.

It's what Rosa Ramirez would do.

Chapter Ten

In the morning, I stay in my room while Max carries his things out to his truck. I don't want to stay away from him, but it's the smart thing to do. Getting over this silly crush is simple—I just have to rip him off quickly, like a Band-Aid. Once he's gone, I can do my interview, then move on with my life. I'll find my writing mojo back tomorrow. I just know I will.

At least, I hope I will.

The rumbly truck engine sound in the driveway means he's already left. I thought he might try to tell me goodbye but then again... I didn't tell him goodbye so I don't know what I expect.

I've been getting ready for my TV interview all morning. The producers told my agent that they'd have someone on site to do my hair and makeup, but I needed to be fresh-faced and have clean hair. And, the worst part of all, I need to dress myself. Sure, I've been dressing myself since I was a toddler, but there's something much different about getting dressed today. I never know what kind of impression I want to make. What kind of author I want to be.

In reality, I live in yoga leggings and baggy T-shirts. In the professional world? Do I wear slacks and a nice shirt? A formal dress? A causal dress?

I've been up since five in the morning trying to figure it out, but eventually I settle on a nice pair of black jeans and a silver shimmery top. Now that Max's truck has left, I emerge from my room to make some coffee.

Only Max's truck hasn't left.

He's standing here with a backpack slung over his shoulder, looking just as surprised to see me as I am to see him.

"I thought you left?" I blurt out like some kind of weirdo.

"I was about to, but someone's here." He peers out the front window. I rush over to look and my arm brushes against his. We're only touching for the teensiest of seconds, but it makes my whole body light up.

"They're here?" I shriek. I'm probably as pale as a

ghost right now. I check my watch. "They're not supposed to be here for two more hours!"

He shrugs. "They're blocking me in. I'll ask them to move."

The TV crew arrived in a big box van thing. My driveway isn't very big, and Max's truck is parked behind my Jeep. Behind him, is the big van. I walk out onto the porch, watching him wave at the guy in cargo shorts and a black Clark TV shirt.

"Hey man, I'm sorry but you're blocking me in and I'm about to leave."

"Oh," the guy says. "Sorry about that."

"Wait!"

A slender woman with long black hair walks around from the back of the van. She's wearing a Bluetooth earpiece and has a MacBook tucked under her arm. She smiles demurely at Max. "Who are you, handsome?"

Max clears his throat. "I'm no one."

The woman looks beyond him, her eyes landing on mine. She bursts into a smile and I recognize her as Tomi, the TV producer for the show. Her photo is in her email signature. Looks like the host of the show, Zoey, isn't here right now. She probably won't arrive until filming begins in a few hours.

"Julie Baskins!" she says with a big grin. "Come here, babe. Let me get a look at you."

I walk down the porch out into the driveway, feeling naked with no makeup on.

Tomi shakes my hand, clasping it in both of her hands as she tells me hello. She smells like cigarettes and fruity perfume. While still holding my hand, she leans in close. "Who is this handsome hunk of man meat?"

"No one," I say, repeating Max's earlier words. "He's just leaving."

Max nods. "Yeah, so if you could move your van, I'll be on my way."

Tomi stares at him, and then at me. "So it's true," she says. Her voice takes a sudden sinister tone which sends a chill down my back.

"What's true?" I say. "He's the guy who remodeled the house and he had to pick up some tools and now he's leaving."

She winks at me. "Got it."

Then she turns to Max. "You stay, hon. I could use your help."

"I don't know—" Max's confusion mirrors mine.

"I'll pay you five thousand dollars to help my crew set up," Tomi says. "Come on. It'll just be an hour or two."

"I appreciate that but—"

My eyes widen and I smack Max in the arm. "Take the job," I say. "It's five thousand dollars!"

He gives me an uncertain look, like he's telling me he'll be happy to leave if I want him to. "You sure?"

"It's five thousand dollars," I say again. "Do it!"

He laughs, running a hand through his hair. "Okay then."

"Wonderful," Tomi says, clapping her hands together once.

The hair and makeup artist's name is Josh. He's covered in colorful tattoos, rocks a hot pink ponytail, and has an Australian accent. I feel wholly uncool compared to this entire TV crew of five people who show up in my house, set up big lights on metal stands, and rearrange my furniture to suit their needs.

Max is put to work helping the crew set up and I catch glimpses of him between Josh doing my hair and makeup, although I'm trying not to stare. Josh styles my shoulder length hair into soft beach curls, twisting two strands of hair near my forehead back and pinning them into place like I'm a fairy princess or something. Then he does my makeup using an air brush which is the coolest thing ever, and then he gives me a soft pink lipstick and subtle smoky eyes.

I look fantastic. I look beautiful. I look—not like

an author, but like a movie star. I wish I could keep Josh forever and have him do my hair and makeup every day.

The new look gives me confidence. I feel great in my shimmery top and jeans, and comfortable enough to wear the high heel suede ankle boots that I never wear outside my house for fear of falling down in them.

When Zoey arrives, she comes with another entourage of her own. Three women dressed impeccably, ready to rush off at a moment's notice to fetch Zoey whatever she needs. I listen to her podcast all the time, but hearing her rich, velvety voice in person leaves me a little star-struck.

She gets right to business. We sit, me on the couch and her on a black leather chair the crew brought for her. They've also moved my bookshelf to be behind me, I guess to make me look extra literary for the interview.

"Julie Baskins," Zoey says, holding out her hands toward me.

"Good morning," I say, hoping my smile looks genuine. "Thank you so much for having me on your show." I am so keenly aware of the big, terrifying camera that's watching me, recording me, that everything I do feels faked and awkward. Like I left my real personality in my bed this morning and now the extra professional version of me is here on the couch.

"You made your mark on the publishing world with your Lucky in Love series, which published seven years ago."

I nod, because it seems like she has more to say.

"But then a few months ago, seemingly out of nowhere, you released a shockingly different type of novel." Zoey holds up a copy of Love Sucks, book one in my new series. She reads the blurb on the cover. "Rosa Ramirez is a kick-butt hero saving heartbroken women one cheating man at a time."

"So," she says, looking pointedly at me. "What made you write the Love Sucks series?"

I give a little shrug. "I wanted something new. When this idea came to me, it sounded fun so I just went with it. Most of my characters in the past were damsels in distress and it's thrilling writing a character who can stand up for herself."

"Hmm," Zoey says, watching me with the untrustworthy eyes of a TV host.

Suddenly I feel like a worm that's been pinned to a board about to be dissected. Zoey's eyes narrow just slightly. "I'm sure I don't have to remind you of the rumors that quickly spread through the literary-gossip-sphere?"

Literary gossip sphere?

"I don't..." I swallow, looking to the coffee table. I thought I had a glass of water. Where's the glass of water?

Zoey smiles. "You were cheated on, Julie. Ouch!" She sucks in air, wincing like she just got pinched. Somehow she manages to still look beautiful while making that face. "I've been there too, lady. Trust me. It's no fun getting cheated on by someone you love."

I try very hard to look impassive. "That's in the past."

"Of course," she says, her smile widening. "You've become a hero to women everywhere. Women who identify with you. As your online biography says, after all, you are anti-romance."

I give a little shrug, glad she's moved on from the cheating ex-boyfriend thing. Jason doesn't deserve even one second of publicity for what he did. "That's me. Feels good to write about something new."

"Do you regret the romance novels that made you a popular author?"

I swallow the knot in my stomach. "Of course not."

"But you are anti-romance now."

"Yes."

Zoey's lips press into a thin smile. A shiver runs down my spine. "Care to explain this?"

She holds up a thick piece of paper, something like a posterboard with an image printed on it. My heart stops. It's not a picture I recognize because I've never seen this. in fact, I didn't know this picture even existed. But it's a picture of me.

And Max.

Smiling at each other like love-struck dorks at Roger's Diner. My hand touches his forearm gingerly, *flirtatiously.*

The bright red light on the camera lens reminds me I'm being recorded right now. Every expression on my face will be aired for everyone to see. How does she expect me to act? Scandalized? Embarrassed? Like some kind of trollop who lies to her fans about being anti-romance and then goes out on dates with hot men?

Well, I'm not going to give her the satisfaction.

"That's Max. He's a friend," I say with a bright, unaffected smile. "Don't tell me you're one of those people who think men and women can't be friends?"

"This looks like much more than friendship," Zoey says, peering at the photo. The photo she'd had professionally printed and bound to a thick posterboard.

This was done specifically to set me up. To air my personal life on camera.

I see red.

I realize that this is my house. I don't have to do anything I don't want to do. So I do the thing Rosa Ramirez would do. I stand up, pulling the mic pack off my shirt with a dramatic flourish.

"You are being extremely rude and this interview is now over."

Chapter Eleven

Tomi swoops in from out of nowhere, trying to smooth things over. With a slice of her hand across her neck, the cameraman turns off the camera. Zoey sits here, back straight, head held high like she's done nothing wrong.

"Julie, please," Tomi says, her earpiece looking like a creepy spider crawling out of her ear. "Don't leave the interview."

"This isn't an interview," I say loudly from the kitchen. This isn't journalism. This is trashy reality TV crap. I didn't sign up for that and I don't have to put up with it."

"You signed up to be interviewed and you didn't specify any topics that were off limits," Tomi says with a smile meant to placate that does absolutely nothing to placate me.

"I didn't know I had to specify off limits questions! I'm an author, not some controversial celebrity!"

Tomi's expression shows she thinks I'm some kind of dumb kid. She opens her mouth to speak again, but then Max steps forward.

"I don't give permission for my image to be used," he says, crossing his arms over his chest.

Tomi winces. "Unfortunately, you don't get to decide that. This picture was taken in a public venue by one of our viewers who sent it in. The law states that public photos in public places are not subject to personal privacy. The only permission we need is that of the photographer, and she's already given it."

"So some stranger creep took a picture of me without me knowing it and I don't get to object?" I glance over toward Zoey, but she's chatting with her beautiful entourage, not seeming the least bit upset that I stopped her interview. It's Tomi the producer begging me to stay.

"Ms. Baskins, that photo is the reason you got this interview. A concerned fan brought it our attention that a prominent author was making money off being against romance, but she was having a romance herself. Your hypocrisy makes for great TV."

"So this was supposed to be some kind of gotcha interview? This is crap, and you know it. Max is my friend. We're not dating." Even as I say the words, I know they're only partially true. He is my friend. And we're NOT dating. But... we kissed. And my crush on him won't go away no matter how much I metaphorically stomp on it in my head.

"That's great," Tomi says. "Totally fine if you're just friends. Go back on the interview and explain that you're just friends. We can edit out the previous few minutes and start over again. That photo will be used to entice viewers, but once they hear your side of the story, it'll all be cleared up. This is actually great publicity for you, Julie."

"I'm only going back on the interview if that picture won't be brought up. I'm here to talk about my books, not my friendships."

Tomi clicks her tongue. "I'm afraid we can't do that."

"What if I join her?" Max says.

My eyes widen and Tomi's nearly pop out of her narrow head. "What?" she says.

"Restart the interview. Bring up the photo. And I'll join Julie on the couch and explain that we're friends. She could even spin this is as something about how authors' lives are in the public view and people try to discredit them. She can turn the interview around into something she approves of." Max looks at me. "What do you think?"

I don't even realize my mouth is open.

Tomi answers for me. "We could do that. I can't prevent Zoey from asking the tough questions, but you can have another shot at how you answer them."

"Okay," I say. My stomach is all butterflies and anxiety like I swallowed a gallon of *what the heck is happening* juice. One glance at Max soothes my nerves. He's magical like that. I nod, more eagerly this time. "Yes. Let's do that."

The interview takes forty-five minutes the second time around. Zoey isn't apologetic. She doesn't even admit that anything went wrong. She gives the interview, and I'm better prepared to rebuff the insinuations that photo gives off, especially with Max at my side. Before I know it, they're packed up and gone.

Now it's just Max and me.

"Thanks for that," I say, hands shoved in my pockets while we watch the van back out of my driveway and leave.

"You look really beautiful."

My head snaps around to him. "Huh?"

"I mean, you're always beautiful. But today... you look really nice, is all."

"It's not me," I say with a snort. "It's the hair and makeup guy's talent, not mine."

"Hair and makeup only helps if you're already beautiful."

I really hope that airbrushed foundation keeps the blush from showing on my cheeks. I could really use a coffee right now, or even a milkshake from Roger's Diner, but after all the awkwardness with Max, I'm not about to ask him to lunch with me. For all I know, more paparazzi could be lurking around, waiting to snap a photo.

"I can't believe they did that to me," I say, exhaling a deep sigh. "I guess it's the only way an author can get fancy interviews like that. No one cares about books unless they can trash the author somehow."

Max shoves his hands in his pockets. He's so much taller than I am, but right now he looks almost like a kid who has had the wind knocked out of his sails. "So is this why you didn't want anything more to happen between us? The anti-romance thing?"

I shrug, my throat feeling like it's full of cotton. "Sort of. I got a huge advance to write these books. I can't be dating men when I'm the face of single women everywhere."

"You can still be an anti-romance author," he says, peering at me through hopeful eyes.

"No," I say with a sarcastic chuckle. "No, I can't. That's the very definition of hypocrisy."

A tiny part of me hopes he'll keep arguing with me, keep trying to convince me to change my mind. Because if I'm being honest, this time with Max has been happier and more fun than any relationship I've ever been in. But he doesn't argue with me. He just nods softly, giving me the smallest little smile.

"Okay," he says. "I understand. Good luck with your books."

And then he's gone.

For real.

Chapter Twelve

Two months later

I read over my editor's email for the third time. It doesn't get any better. Turns out reading it yet again doesn't somehow change the meaning of the words she used. She doesn't like my new Love Sucks manuscript. She thinks Rosa Ramirez is too bitter, the plot is too slow, and the characters are cliché. To put it simply, the next Love Sucks book, well, sucks.

I can't blame her, either. I sped through this book without putting the care into it that I usually do. Partly because I was running late on meeting my deadline, but there's another reason, too. A bigger, elephant-sized reason.

That reason has dirty blond hair and honey-brown eyes.

With a sigh, I close my email.

My best friend Annie was supposed to come spend the weekend with me but then she got called to cover a shift for her coworker so now I'm stuck hanging out all by myself with just my loneliness and misery to keep me company. This is not how things were supposed to work.

I was supposed to be happy here in Sterling. I was supposed to be free to write all the novels and gain all the fame and notoriety that comes with being anti-romance. I should have been happy. It should have been easy.

Now I feel even more alone than when I lived just across the hallway from my ex and his new girlfriend. The lake in my back yard isn't as beautiful when I'm grumpy all day.

This problem with my editor won't go away no matter how much I ignore it, but a girl's gotta eat, after all, so I leave the email unanswered and head to Roger's Diner.

The Saturday lunch crowd packs the place but I arrive just in time to slide into a small two-person table that overlooks the water. The spunky blonde waitress is named Claire, and she's become one of my very few friends here in Sterling. Probably because I visit almost every day. I can't help it. The food is too good and too cheap to stay away.

"Is it fun eating your soda and junk food without healthy boy Max here?" she says with a snort when I order a milkshake to go with my cheese fries.

"Oh yes," I say grinning as I grab a cheesy fry and pop it in my mouth. "I like not having to look at salads."

She chuckles. "Is he off renovating another house? When will he be back?"

I shrug. "I don't know."

She hovers, like she wants to keep talking. "Wait a minute..." she pulls a pen from the bun on top of her head, scratching something on her order pad. "Are you telling me you let that man leave your house without plans to meet up again?"

"We weren't really friends," I say, eating another fry. "We only met because my landlady has no idea how to schedule her tenants correctly."

"Oh, honey," Claire says, shaking her head and smacking her lips. "You act like meeting him was some random coincidence."

"It was?" I lift an eyebrow. What else could it be?

She shakes her head. "No way, lady. The Universe doesn't just throw things together for the fun of it. You met him on purpose. You're perfect for him."

I snort out a laugh. "No, I'm not. I don't even date. I'm done with men."

"I know he misses you," she says with a hint of smirk in her smile.

"All I did was annoy him," I say, shrugging off her words. "I bet he's glad to be rid of me."

"Aww, sweetie." She picks up my menu, tucking it under her arm. "You don't believe a word of that."

I want to argue with her, to tell her that yes of course I believe it because it's true because Max and I were just temporary roommates and that's all, and that's all it'll ever be because I'm Julie Baskins, the anti-romance author of the best-selling Love Sucks series.

She tears off the paper on her order pad before I can say any of that and places it on the table in front of me. In her loopy handwriting, she's written the name Max, and then a phone number.

"That's his business number," she says, tapping it with a pink fingernail. "That's how I have it memorized... we call him all the time for fixing stuff around the diner. But he's the only one who answers that phone so give him a call if you want." She winks at me before walking away.

I eat my fries and sip my milkshake and look out at the water as if I don't care one bit about the piece of paper in front of me.

But when a breeze blows across the patio, I reach out quickly and stop it from floating away.

Annie gives me a puzzled look while she takes a bite of her sandwich. She's been working a double at the hospital but now that it's her lunch break we're video chatting. I just broke the news to her that my editor hates my new manuscript and my life is probably over

"You're being a little dramatic," Annie says over a mouthful of food. "I doubt your career is *over*."

"She hates it." I lean back on my couch, letting my hair fan out on the pillow behind me and then blow a raspberry sigh. "She hates it. She didn't even have any suggestions for how to make it better. She just hates it."

Annie rolls her eyes. "So what happens now?"

"I'm not sure." I gaze up at the crisp white ceiling. The ceiling that Max and I painted together. "I have to send her something because the publishing house has already paid me for the next book in my series and I've already spent all of that money. I need something."

"You could write a brand new book," Annie suggests. "If that one you sent her is so bad maybe just write a new one?"

"The thing is…" I chew on my lip and think about the folded piece of paper in my back pocket. "I'm not sure I can write another Love Sucks story."

Annie frowns. "Why not?"

"Maybe…" I take a deep breath. I think Annie might have a slight idea that maybe what I'm about to say is true, but we haven't officially talked about it. "Maybe I don't have as much enthusiasm for the anti-romance thing as I used to."

"Hmm," she says. She opens a string cheese and then bites the top right off it like some kind of cheese-eating monster.

"Did you just decapitate your string cheese?"

She glances down at it and shrugs, taking another bite.

"You're supposed to peel them into strings," I say, with a sarcastically horrified expression.

"I live on the wild side," she says, wiggling her eyebrows as she takes another bite."

I shake my head. "So ruthless."

"Stop trying to change the subject, Jules. I think we both know the solution to your problem."

She looks at me as if she expects me to finish her

train of thought for her, but I'm blank. Clearly, we both don't know the solution to the problem.

"If you have a solution, I'd be happy to hear it."

Annie rolls her eyes. "Write with your heart."

I stick my tongue out and make a gagging sound. "Bad advice. Worst advice ever. Hearts have nothing to do with business."

"Yeah, maybe if your business is being a banker or something. But your heart has everything to do with your writing, Julie. I've known you forever. I know how you operate. You write how you feel, even if it's subtle. And when you were pissed and angry at Jason, you wrote Love Sucks. Now you're over that cheating loser and you've got feelings for someone else and you can't hold the same enthusiasm as before."

I sit up straight. "You are imagining things, babe. I don't have feelings for anyone except maybe my coffee maker because it's glorious. That thing can brew my coffee any day."

She snorts. "Fine, deny it. Pretend you don't totally have the hots for the hottie renovation guy you talked about constantly while he was there. I'm your best friend, so I'll just pretend right along with you if that's what you want. But if you ever want to come back to reality and accept the truth, then I'll give you this advice: Write what you feel. It's never let you down before."

Her words are so profound they leave me speechless for a moment. Then her phone alarm goes off and she curses under her breath. "Crap! Gotta get back to work. Love ya!"

And then she's gone, and I'm staring at my phone's home screen. And I get an idea. It's crazy and wild and might be a total disaster, but it's an idea, and it's more than I had a few minutes ago.

But before I can implement that idea, I need to get everything out in the open.

Max's voicemail picks up after several rings. *"You've reached Spenser Construction. Sorry I'm not available to take your call but please leave me a detailed message and I'll call you back as soon as I can."*

"Hey Max, it's Julie. Call me back? Thanks."

<h1 style="text-align:center">Chapter Thirteen</h1>

Since I can't focus on my terrible manuscript, I walk down to the lake. Just a few blocks away is a public park with picnic tables, a playground, and a sandy shore where the locals go swimming. I'm a little terrified of water and would rather admire the lake's beauty from the solid ground, but since I'm in desperate need of something to take my mind off my career and Max, I slip off my sandals and sink my toes into the water's edge.

My phone rings from the back pocket of my denim shorts. I suck in a short breath. I'm not sure I'm mentally capable of handling things if it's my agent calling to ream me out for turning in such a terrible manuscript. Everything I've worked so hard for might fall apart with one phone call if my publisher decides to dump me and demand their book advance money back.

The phone keeps ringing, and I know I'll have to look at it eventually. I brace myself for the worst.

It's Max.

Now my heartbeat is even more erratic.

"Hey," I answer. My teeth dig into my bottom lip as I gaze out at the sparkling lake in front of me.

"What's wrong? Did something break?"

"Huh?"

"I got your message... that you need to talk to me. Please tell me I didn't royally screw up something in the renovations. I knew working quickly might cause a problem, but I'm pretty sure I was thorough in all my repairs..."

"No, no it's not the house." My throat tightens. Max thought I was calling about the house, not about him. About us. About the spark of something between us that I really hope we can explore further. Maybe I should just let it go. Tell him never mind and end the call and go back to my life as a single woman, happy or not.

"Ah, so you missed me." I can hear his smile through the phone.

I roll my eyes. "You wish."

"Well if it's not the house and you didn't miss me, then what is it?"

Dang. I exhale loudly. "I guess maybe it's one of the two."

"Where are you?"

"Sterling Park, by the shore and the blue picnic tables."

"Don't go anywhere," he says. Then he hangs up.

Twenty minutes pass with me standing here, milling about, checking my phone and wondering if I've been weirdly set up. Then I spot Max walking up the shore toward me.

All the anxious butterflies in my stomach metaphorically wake up and fly around, making me even more nervous. I'm prepared for awkward silences and discomfort—we didn't exactly leave things happy and fun the last time we spoke. As he nears, he smiles. His stubble has grown out longer than I've seen before and he looks rugged, sexy, and absolutely delicious. He's tanner, too, I think, which has made his hair a little more blond.

I smile back, giving him a little wave. I'm not sure what to say? Oh gosh, what do I say?

Nothing, as it turns out.

Max's lips are on mine before I can utter a word. I breathe him in, feel his strong, calloused hands slip around my waist and pull me to him with an almost painful ferocity. I tangle my hands in his hair. My toes lift out of the sand.

I'm breathless, caught up in this moment, in this kiss, which is somehow even better than the first one we shared on my back porch. Maybe because this time it's not just a one-time spontaneous thing. This time it's real.

This time it's permanent.

When our lips break apart, Max's forehead presses to mine. His grin lights up my vision, his breath fresh and minty. "Hi," he breathes.

"Hi," I say back.

"I'm glad you called."

"I'm glad you kissed me."

He laughs, lowering me back to the sand but keeping his arms around me.

"You're all I've thought about, Julie. Every single day. No matter what I'm doing, or how busy I am with work, it's just you. My brain thinks of only you."

"But why?" I ask, reality sinking back in now that there's a few inches of space between us and I can think better. "Is this infatuation or...something real?"

"I don't do infatuation," he says, reaching up and taking my hands in his. "I've been in this small town my entire life. I've never connected with anyone like I connected with you. I don't want to lose that. I don't want to lose you. What I feel for you is as real as anything."

I may not be a private investigator myself, but everything in his voice, his expression, and his eyes tells me he's being truthful. That he's not just filling his time with me until someone better comes along. Can I do that, too? Can I allow myself to trust him, to trust in us, and find happiness again?

Or will I always be worried that something bad is lurking around the corner?

"Please tell me you feel the same." Max squeezes my hands. "We can keep the whole thing a secret if that's what's best for your career. I just want to be with you, in any way that you'll have me."

"I don't want you to be a secret," I say.

He grins. "Does that mean you want me?"

"What do you think?" I wrap my arms around his neck and pull him in for another kiss.

It's eight in the morning and I'm not even tired. Max brings me another cup of coffee before settling next to me on the couch again. "Do you have a title yet?"

I yawn, stretching my hands into the air before

putting them back on my laptop. Okay, maybe I am a *little* tired. My body wants sleep but my brain just wants to keep on truckin'. I've just pulled an all-nighter. Max slept next to me on my couch, his feet propped up on the coffee table. He'd listened to me tell him about my newest manuscript and how much my editor hated it. He'd gotten extremely cocky when I told him that my writing has suffered ever since I met him because it's hard to write about hating romance when I was feeling very romantic toward him.

Then he'd encouraged me to write what I wanted to write, and when the idea hit me, he'd stayed right next to me as I typed away all night long, writing the first five chapters of my new novel. Twenty thousand words in one night. It's a record. It's a miracle.

With any luck, it'll save my career.

"I don't have an official title yet," I say, scrolling back to the top of my document. "Right now I'm calling it: *Love Sucks Book 2 – the one where P.I. Rosa Ramirez finds love again.*"

"I'm no book expert, but it sounds great." He leans over, kissing me on the cheek.

"This is amazing coffee," I say, taking a big sip.

"Have you been awake all night?" he asks.

"Yep. You sleep like an angel, by the way."

He blushes. "I'm pretty sure I sleep like a sexy man."

I roll my eyes. "Nope. Pretty angelic."

He cups my face in his hands, gently bringing ours lips together. My whole body lights up at his kiss. A girl could really get used to this.

"You should really get some sleep."

I nod, yawning again. "Right after I send this to my editor...." I type up the email, attach my new draft, and send it.

"Let's get you to bed and I'll come see you later today." Max starts to stand but I hold him back.

"You don't have anything going on today, do you?"

"Nope."

"Great," I say, handing him the TV remote. "Let me just take a little nap." I snuggle against his chest and close my eyes. He's a little too muscular to make a good pillow, but I'm too tired to care. "Then in a few hours we can head to the diner for lunch."

"And we can get a nice healthy salad to give you back all the energy you just used pulling an all-nighter?"

"Nope," I say, grinning as I pull a throw blanket over me. "I'm thinking nachos."

He chuckles, running his hand through my hair. "And a milkshake?"

"Obviously."

He kisses me softly on the forehead. The imaginary Rosa Ramirez in my mind winks at me. I don't hate romance. Not anymore.

In fact, I think love it.

About the Author

Amy Sparling is the bestselling author of books for teens and the teens at heart. She lives on the coast of Texas with her family, her spoiled rotten pets, and a huge pile of books. She graduated with a degree in English and has worked at a bookstore, coffee shop, and a fashion boutique. Her fashion skills aren't the best, but luckily she turned her love of coffee and books into a writing career that means she can work in her pajamas. Her favorite things are coffee, book boyfriends, and Netflix binges.

She's always loved reading books from R. L. Stine's Fear Street series, to The Baby Sitter's Club series by Ann, Martin, and of course, Twilight. She started writing her own books in 2010 and now publishes several books a year. Amy loves getting messages from her readers and responds to every single one! Connect with her on one of the links below.

www.AmySparling.com